Matthew A.   Matthew B.   Matthew C.

Peter Catalanotto

Matthew
A.B.C.

A Richard Jackson Book   Atheneum Books for Young Readers

New York   London   Toronto   Sydney   Singapore

For Esmé

Atheneum Books for Young Readers

An imprint of Simon & Schuster Children's Publishing Division

1230 Avenue of the Americas

New York, New York 10020

Book design by Michael Nelson

The text of this book is set in Lemonade Bold.

The illustrations are rendered in watercolor.

Printed in Hong Kong

First Edition

2 4 6 8 10 9 7 5 3

Library of Congress Cataloging-in-Publication Data

Catalanotto, Peter.

Matthew A.B.C. / Peter Catalanotto.

p. cm.

"A Richard Jackson book."

Summary: A new boy named Matthew joins Mrs. Tuttle's class, which already has twenty-five students whose first names are Matthew and whose last names begin with every letter except Z.

ISBN 0-689-84582-0

[1. Names, Personal—Fiction. 2. Identity—Fiction. 3. Schools—Fiction. 4. Alphabet] I. Title.

PZ7.C26878 Mat 2002

[E]—dc21   2001022986

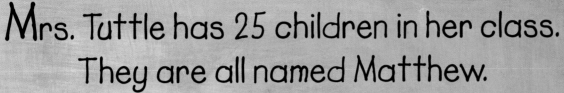

Mrs. Tuttle has 25 children in her class.
They are all named Matthew.

Principal Nozzet wonders how
Mrs. Tuttle tells them apart.

She finds it quite simple.

Bb

Matthew B. loves Band-Aids.

Matthew C.
has friendly cowlicks.

Cc

Dd

Matthew D.
believes he's a duck.

Ee

Matthew E. forgets how to eat.

Ff

Matthew F. has a cat on his face.

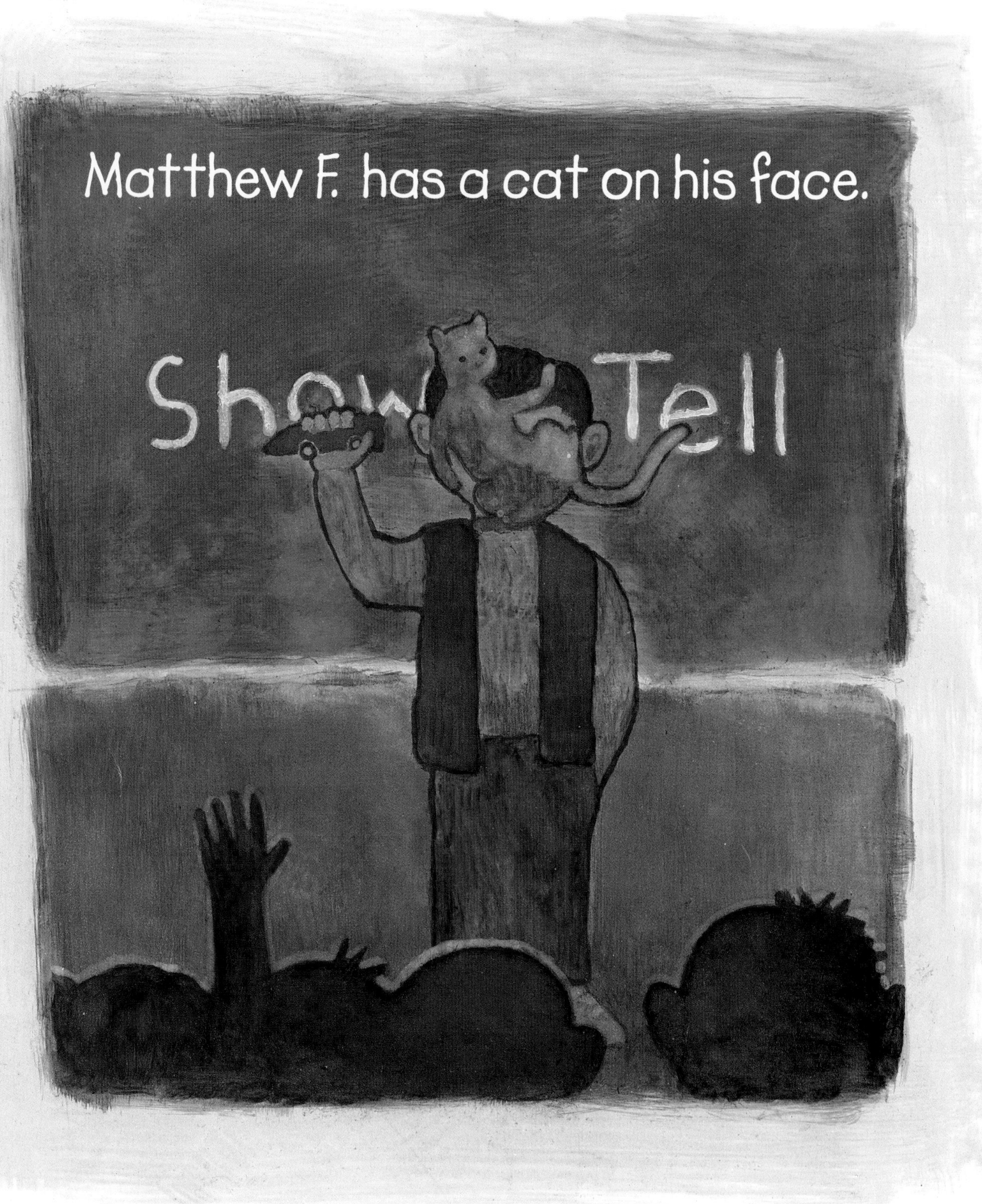

Jj

Matthew J.
works a night job.

Matthew K.
is unusually fond of ketchup.

Kk

Matthew L.
leaks.

Nn

Matthew N. is nearly naked.

Matthew O.
stays outside.

Pp

Matthew P. is perpetually perplexed.

Matthew Q.
is queasy.

Qq

Ss

Matthew S.
can't wait for summer.

Matthew U. is completely uneven.

Matthew W.
has a very high waist.

Ww

Matthew X. swallowed the xylophone.

Yy

Matthew Y. only yodels.

SHOW AND ~~TELL~~

YODEL

Principal Nozzet tells Mrs. Tuttle
she has a new student.

His name is . . .

Matthew.

Zz

Mrs. Tuttle sees he is
exactly what her class needs.

MATTHEW ZEE